A Note to Parents and Caregivers:

Read-it! Readers are for children who are just starting on the amazing road to reading. These beautiful books support both the acquisition of reading skills and the love of books.

The RED LEVEL presents familiar topics using common words and repeating sentence patterns.

The BLUE LEVEL presents new ideas using a larger vocabulary and varied sentence structure.

The YELLOW LEVEL presents more challenging ideas, a broad vocabulary, and wide variety in sentence structure.

The GREEN LEVEL presents more complex ideas, an extended vocabulary range, and expanded language structures.

When sharing a book with your child, read in short stretches, pausing often to talk about the pictures. Have your child turn the pages and point to the pictures and familiar words. And be sure to reread favorite stories or parts of stories.

There is no right or wrong way to share books with children. Find time to read with your child, and pass on the legacy of literacy.

Adria F. Klein, Ph.D.
Professor Emeritus
California State University
San Bernardino, California

Managing Editor: Bob Temple
Creative Director: Terri Foley
Editor: Brenda Haugen
Editorial Adviser: Andrea Cascardi
Copy Editor: Laurie Kahn
Designer: Melissa Voda
Page production: The Design Lab
The illustrations in this book were rendered in watercolor and pencil.

Picture Window Books
5115 Excelsior Boulevard
Suite 232
Minneapolis, MN 55416
1-877-845-8392
www.picturewindowbooks.com

Printed in the United States of America.

Library of Congress Cataloging-in-Publication Data
Blair, Eric.
The Bremen town musicians / by Jacob and Wilhelm Grimm ; by Eric Blair ;
illustrated by Bill Dickson.
p. cm. — (Read-it! readers fairy tales)
Summary: While on their way to Bremen, four aging animals who are no longer of any
use to their masters find a new home after outwitting a gang of robbers.
ISBN 1-4048-0310-6 (Library Binding)
[1. Fairy tales. 2. Folklore—Germany.] I. Grimm, Jacob, 1785-1863. II. Grimm,
Wilhelm, 1786-1859. III. Dickson, Bill, 1949- ill. IV. Bremen town musicians. English.
V. Title. VI. Series.
PZ8.B5688Br 2004
398.2—dc22   2003014007

The Bremen Town Musicians

A Retelling of the Grimms' Fairy Tale
By Eric Blair

Illustrated by Bill Dickson

Content Adviser:
Kathy Baxter, M.A.
Former Coordinator of Children's Services
Anoka County (Minnesota) Library

Reading Advisers:
Adria F. Klein, Ph.D.
Professor Emeritus, California State University
San Bernardino, California

Susan Kesselring, M.A.
Literacy Educator
Rosemount-Apple Valley-Eagan (Minnesota) School District

Picture Window Books
Minneapolis, Minnesota

About the Brothers Grimm

To help a friend, brothers Jacob and Wilhelm Grimm began collecting old stories told in their home country of Germany. Events in their lives would take the brothers away from their project, but they never forgot about it. Several years later, the Grimms published their first books of fairy tales. The stories they collected still are enjoyed by children and adults today.

Once upon a time, there was a weak old donkey. His owner decided to get rid of him.

The donkey knew what his owner was thinking. The donkey decided to run away to save himself. He left for Bremen to join the town band.

On the road, the donkey met an old dog.

The dog said, "I'm too old to hunt.
My master wants to get rid of me.
What should I do?"

"Come with me," the donkey said.
"I'm on my way to join the Bremen
Town Band. I can play the lute.
You can bang the drums."

The donkey and the dog went down
the road together.

Soon they met a sad old cat. "What's the matter?" asked the donkey.

"My mistress tried to drown me," said the cat. "I'm too old to chase mice. I just want to sit by the fire and purr. Where should I go?"

9

"Come along with us," said the donkey.
"The band can use a cat who sings."

So the cat joined the dog and the donkey.

Then the animals met a rooster.
The rooster was sitting on a farmer's gate.
"Cock-a-doodle-doo," the rooster
crowed sadly.

"What a horrible sound!" said the donkey.
"What's wrong?"

"I'm having a good crow while I still can," said the rooster. "My mistress told the cook to put me in the soup. What should I do?"

"Anyplace is better than the soup pot,"
said the donkey. "Come along with us."

So the donkey, the dog, the cat, and
the rooster went together down the road
toward Bremen.

BREMEN

Night came. The animals
stopped in the forest to rest.
The rooster flew high into a tree.
He saw lights from a house.

"That would be a much
better place to sleep," said
the donkey. The animals walked
to the house.

14

The animals peeked in the window.
They saw a table covered with food.
A band of robbers sat enjoying dinner.

The animals came up with a plan
to chase the robbers from the house.

The donkey stood with his front feet
against the window. The dog jumped
onto the donkey's back. The cat climbed
onto the dog. The rooster flew up
onto the cat's neck.

They quietly counted together: "Three, two, one." Then, all at once, the donkey brayed, the dog barked, the cat meowed, and the rooster crowed.

The noisy animals crashed through the window.

The frightened robbers ran out
of the house and into the forest.

The animals sat down at the table and ate the robbers' dinner. When the animals finished eating, they turned out the lights and went to sleep.

19

The robbers were watching the house from the forest. They saw the lights go out.

The robbers' leader ordered one of his men to go back to the house and look around.

The robber sneaked into the dark house.
He saw the cat's fiery red eyes. He thought
they were burning coals from the fireplace.

The cat jumped at the robber's face
and began spitting and scratching.

The robber ran for the back door. The dog jumped up and bit him on the leg.

As the robber dashed through the yard, the donkey kicked him. The rooster shrieked, "Cock-a-doodle-doo!"

24

The robber ran for his life. He went back to the forest and told his leader what had happened.

"First a terrible witch hissed at me.
She scratched me with her long nails!"
said the robber.

"Then a man came from behind the door. He stabbed me in the leg with a sharp knife!"

"Then a monster beat me while a judge screamed, 'Bring me the rascal!'" the robber said. "I ran away as fast as I could. It's not safe in there."

29

The robbers never came back to the house. The four animals of the Bremen Town Band loved their new home. They stayed there and lived happily ever after.

Levels for *Read-it!* Readers

Read-it! Readers help children practice early reading skills
with brightly illustrated stories.

Red Level: Familiar topics with frequently used words and
repeating patterns.

Blue Level: New ideas with a larger vocabulary and a variety
of language structures.

Little Red Riding Hood, by Maggie Moore 1-4048-0064-6

The Three Little Pigs, by Maggie Moore 1-4048-0071-9

Yellow Level: Challenging ideas with an expanded vocabulary
and a wide variety of sentences.

Cinderella, by Barrie Wade 1-4048-0052-2

Goldilocks and the Three Bears, by Barrie Wade 1-4048-0057-3

Jack and the Beanstalk, by Maggie Moore 1-4048-0059-X

The Three Billy Goats Gruff, by Barrie Wade 1-4048-0070-0

Green Level: More complex ideas with an extended vocabulary
range and expanded language structures.

The Brave Little Tailor, by Eric Blair 1-4048-0315-7

The Bremen Town Musicians, by Eric Blair 1-4048-0310-6

The Emperor's New Clothes, by Susan Blackaby 1-4048-0224-X

The Fisherman and His Wife, by Eric Blair 1-4048-0317-3

The Frog Prince, by Eric Blair 1-4048-0313-0

Hansel and Gretel, by Eric Blair 1-4048-0316-5

The Little Mermaid, by Susan Blackaby 1-4048-0221-5

The Princess and the Pea, by Susan Blackaby 1-4048-0223-1

Rumpelstiltskin, by Eric Blair 1-4048-0311-4

The Shoemaker and His Elves, by Eric Blair 1-4048-0314-9

Snow White, by Eric Blair 1-4048-0312-2

The Steadfast Tin Soldier, by Susan Blackaby 1-4048-0226-6

Thumbelina, by Susan Blackaby 1-4048-0225-8

The Ugly Duckling, by Susan Blackaby 1-4048-0222-3